The Girl AND THE MIRROR

Written by Alberto Monnar

Illustrated by Lisa Morton

First published by
Readers Are Leaders U.S.A.
March 6, 2008

The Girl and the Mirror
Written by Alberto Monnar
Illustrated by Lisa Morton
Edited by Linda Weinerman
Interior lay-out design by Masha Shubin

ISBN
0-9768035-8-5

ISBN 13
978-0-9768035-8-4

Please visit us @
www.monnar.net
www.ExpressYourself101.net
www.ReadersAreLeadersUSA.net

Readers Are Leaders U.S.A.
Founded in 2002
Miami, Florida

It was dark, and Britney was very fearful.

Britney, who was 14 years old, thought that she was the prettiest girl in the world. Very frequently, she would gaze into the mirror and think she saw perfection. Britney was conceited and arrogant. Days, weeks, months, and years passed and Britney still had those characteristics.

Her mother was very patient and explained that beauty was not all in life. Kindness, sympathy, compassion, and consideration to others are the key to happiness. Determination and tenacity are the ingredients when it comes to studies and goals in life in order to succeed. Britney would see her mother moving her mouth, but the advice went in one ear, and out the other. Until one day when her world was turned inside out.

It started after school when she had a fight with her boyfriend because he refused to carry all of her belongings. He would usually carry her stuff around because he was madly in love. Her beauty was what attracted him to her from the second he met her, plus he cared for her spunkiness also. But after a while of her being so demanding, pushy, arrogant, and conceited, he grew tired of it. He felt weary, and very exhausted. He continuously had to prove himself to her by answering to her demands just to please her. The more he did the less satisfied she was. As they fought he told her, "Unless you decide to change, I don't want to be your boyfriend anymore!" But Britney didn't believe in changing.

At that moment, Britney decided to go for a walk to cool down. As it started to get dark she noticed a pathway. It led to where she had never been before. As Britney walked she realized that the passageway led to her house. As it grew darker she also recognized that she was in the middle of nowhere—lost, hungry, and thirsty. Britney's day was not going well at all.

"What should I do if I'm lost and lonely while everyone should be doing what I want instead?"

She opened her bag to see if there was any food but there was nothing. As Britney searched inside her bag, she found her mirror, viewed herself, and then smiled. She smiled like never before, and after that, she said to herself, "I am the best thing that happened to this world and I shouldn't be scared." Next she decided to sing and she sang for about an hour. It was almost midnight as she wondered why her parents hadn't looked for her yet.

The whole day was going very strangely for Britney. Britney's watch beeped at midnight, and by that time she was very aggravated. She wished she had never walked that path. However, something about that path was mystical, magical, and spiritual. As she was thinking why, she heard a noise close to her. It was made by a man around 40 years of age. He scared Britney half to death.

"Umm, are you ok?" Britney asked, but the man did not answer.

She got closer and looked into his face, which was half torn off and scared her even more. She kept telling herself she wanted to go home but didn't know how to.

The man then opened his eyes and mumbled," Britney, you cannot get out!"

Then she asked, "Why is that?"

The man then got closer and with a deep voice answered, "You made a huge mistake during your lifetime and now you are stuck and cannot leave. You will stay here forever and there is nothing you can do about it!" As the man's voice became louder and louder she was thinking about the sequence of events that happened throughout her life. At that exact moment she thought her life would end right there.

As Britney went to sit next to the tree she noticed herself in the mirror again. She smiled but the mirror cracked within seconds and she cried.

Britney then said to herself, "What have I done? I am a failure."

In a matter of seconds she wished she had changed when everyone told her to. This whole experience made her think a lot. She just wanted to be home.

As the man spoke again he said, "Now your time is over."

Britney was so confused. Suddenly she noticed a group of people walking towards her. She looked to see their faces and the first person she saw was her mom. Britney then viewed her own face in the mirror, and it was destroyed and she was ugly. Next she saw the other people, and they were people whom she had made fun of—from nerds to her boyfriend. Britney glanced at the mirrors and saw the ugliest thing in the world. As she looked at her reflection it was not her face she saw now; instead she saw beyond, right through to her personality. Britney was shocked to see herself and then realized that everyone who had previously been around her had become prettier. She really couldn't believe that all of this was happening to her.

She cried and cried and then saw her boyfriend. As she walked up to him she asked, "What have I done?"

There was no answer but her boyfriend just looked up to her face and he had tears in his eyes. She looked back at the man and inquired, "What is happening to me?" Then she heard a loud noise and the ground shook as if there was an earthquake. The group of people that were there, started to walk around her. But this time each of them had a mirror and pointed it at her. She was so scared she closed her eyes.

When Britney opened her eyes again she saw that she had only been dreaming. In tears she walked up to her mom's room, opened the door and gave her a hug. She looked into her eyes and saw that her mom was actually the most beautiful thing she had ever seen. Her mom was shocked with her daughter's behavior and started crying too.

"I wish your dad could have seen you like this, Britney."

During lunchtime, Britney sat happily with the nerds and talked very pleasantly to them. All the teachers were looking with amazement.

As school ended she gave a kiss on the cheek to her boyfriend and started to walk home. On her walk she noticed a man who was sitting down near a place that looked very familiar to her. On closer approach she saw the man looking at her. Then the man gave her a smile, which shocked her. She started crying as she realized that this man was the same one from her dream.

When she started to wipe away the tears, the man sitting down disappeared. She felt as if she did the right thing and changed her whole life for the better. For the next two days Britney was overwhelmed by all the changes in her life. She decided to sit on a bench. As she sat down she felt something in her bag. This time as she took out the mirror she couldn't believe what she saw. She just stared at herself for hours because she saw the prettiest thing in the world. However, this time it didn't show how she looked, but showed how good of a person she actually was, and that is the most beautiful thing you can see while looking at a mirror.

CPSIA information can be obtained
at www.ICGtesting.com
Printed in the USA
LVHW070402170721
692927LV00001B/32